**USING THIS BOOK**

*Children learn to read by **reading**, but they need help to begin.*

*When you have read the story on the left-hand pages aloud to the child, go back to the beginning of the book and look at the pictures together.*

*Encourage children to read the sentences under the pictures. If they don't know a word, give them a chance to "guess" what it is from the illustrations before telling them.*

There are more suggestions for helping children learn to read in the *Parent/Teacher Guide.*

© Text and layout SHEILA McCULLAGH MCMLXXXV
© In publication LADYBIRD BOOKS LTD MCMLXXXV
Loughborough, England
LADYBIRD BOOKS, INC.
Lewiston, Maine 04240 U.S.A.

Printed in England

# The Little Monster

*written by* SHEILA McCULLAGH
*illustrated by* GAVIN ROWE

This book belongs to:

Ladybird Books

The Griffle lived in the garden
of the old house in Puddle Lane.
The Griffle was a green monster,
and he could vanish
when he wanted to.
He was a little nervous,
but he was very friendly,
and he liked the children
who lived in Puddle Lane.

The Griffle lived in the garden
of the old house.

Sarah lived in Puddle Lane.
One day, she went out.
The sun was shining, and
the sky was blue.
Sarah went up the lane
to the garden of the old house.

Sarah lived in Puddle Lane.
She went up the lane
to the garden
of the old house.

She looked into the garden,
and she saw the Griffle.
"Hello, Griffle," said Sarah.
She opened the gate,
and went into the garden.

She looked into the garden,
and she saw the Griffle.
She went into the garden.

The Griffle had been feeling lonely,
and he was very glad to see Sarah.
They began to play hide-and-seek.
Sarah hid first.
She hid behind a tree,
but the Griffle soon found her.

The Griffle was glad
to see Sarah.
Sarah played with the Griffle.

Then it was the Griffle's turn to hide.
There was a very old tree
in a corner of the garden.
The tree was hollow.
The Griffle hid inside the hollow tree.
He vanished, but he left his tail showing
so that Sarah could see him.

There was an old tree
in the garden.
The Griffle hid
in the old tree.

Sarah looked for the Griffle.
She looked in the bushes,
and she looked by the house.
She looked by the wall,
and she looked by the gate.
But she didn't see the Griffle.

Sarah looked for the Griffle.
She looked in the bushes,
and she looked by the house.
She looked by the wall,
and she looked by the gate.
But she didn't see the Griffle.

Sarah went to the old tree.
She looked in the old tree,
but she didn't see the Griffle's tail.
(The Griffle was green,
and so was his tail,
so it didn't show up very well.)

Sarah went to the old tree.
She looked in the old tree,
but she didn't see
the Griffle's tail.

Sarah had just gone past the tree,
when she heard a great shout.
It was something like a yell,
and something like a roar.
It came from the hollow tree.
Sarah ran back to the tree.

Sarah ran back to the tree.

She was just in time to see the Griffle.
The Griffle jumped out of the hollow tree,
as if the tree was on fire!

She saw the Griffle.
The Griffle jumped out
of the tree.

But the tree wasn't on fire.
It looked just as it always did.
Sarah stood still, staring.
She looked at the tree, and
she looked at the Griffle.
The Griffle landed on the grass
and turned to look at her.
He looked very frightened.

Sarah looked at the tree, and
she looked at the Griffle.

"Whatever is the matter, Griffle?"
asked Sarah.
The Griffle was shaking like a leaf.
"There's a m – m – monster in the tree,"
said the Griffle, "a little monster."
"What kind of monster?" asked Sarah.

"There is a monster
in the tree," said the Griffle.
"There is a little monster
in the tree."

"I think **you** call it a mouse,"
said the Griffle.

"A mouse!" said Sarah.

"A mouse isn't a monster.
It's a lovely little creature.
A mouse won't hurt you.
I like mice."

"I hate mice," said the Griffle.

"They frighten me."

"A mouse!" said Sarah.
"I like mice."
"I hate mice," said the Griffle.

Sarah went to the old tree,
and looked in.
A little mouse was sitting
inside the tree.
He was nibbling an acorn.

Sarah went to the old tree,
and looked in.

Sarah bent down, and
gently picked up the little mouse.
"I'll put him outside in the lane,"
she said, turning toward the Griffle.
"Then we can go on playing."

Sarah picked up the mouse.
"I will put the mouse
in the lane," she said.

"No, we can't," said the Griffle.
"Where there is one mouse,
there are bound to be more.
I'll come back another day."
The Griffle vanished.

The Griffle vanished.

x

Sarah looked at the little mouse.
He didn't seem at all frightened.
He sat on Sarah's hand.
He looked very thin.
"I'll take you home," said Sarah.
"I'll find some cheese for you."
She put the little mouse
in her pocket, and
went out of the gate
into Puddle Lane.

The mouse sat on Sarah's hand.
"I will take you home,"
said Sarah.
She put the little mouse
in her pocket.

She hadn't gone very far,
when she met Mrs. Pitter-Patter.
"Sarah," said Mrs. Pitter-Patter,
"take your hand out of your pocket.
You should **never** walk along
with your hands in your pockets."

Sarah met Mrs. Pitter-Patter
in Puddle Lane.
Mrs. Pitter-Patter said,
"Take your hand
out of your pocket."

"But I have a mouse in my pocket,
Mrs. Pitter-Patter," said Sarah.
She took the little mouse
out of her pocket,
and opened her hand.

Sarah took the little mouse
out of her pocket.

Mrs. Pitter-Patter screamed
almost as loudly
as the Griffle had roared.
She jumped up in the air,
and turned around.
She ran home down Puddle Lane
as fast as she could.

Mrs. Pitter-Patter ran home
as fast as she could.

"She must be afraid of mice, too,"
said Sarah.
She looked at the little mouse.
He was sitting on her hand, and
combing his whiskers with his paws.
"I don't know why anyone
would be afraid of you," said Sarah.
"I will take you home, and
give you some supper.
Then I will put you back
in the old tree."

Sarah looked at the little mouse.
The little mouse sat
on her hand.
"I will take you home,"
said Sarah.

*This is one of several stories in **Stage 2** about the Griffle. All the books in each Stage are separate stories and are written at the same reading level. It is important for children to read as many books as possible in each Stage before going on to the next Stage.*

Mr. Gotobed